The Monst[er] of My Head!

Written by Valerie Stavey Illustrated by Josef Hoff

For Brabbybear and Sizabear - vs
For Adibear - jh

Most of the time

I'm a kid who has fun!

I laugh

and I play

and I ride

and I run.

My teachers all like me;

I do well in school.

I finish my homework and follow the rules.

But once in a while, I'm caught by surprise,

and I feel something
go from my toes
to my eyes!

and sometimes
I'm fine -
I can just let it go.

When Mom doesn't
let me stay outside
with friends,

or Sissy takes all of

my best drawing pens,

or with turning around and just walking away.

But other times
when nothing seems
to go right,

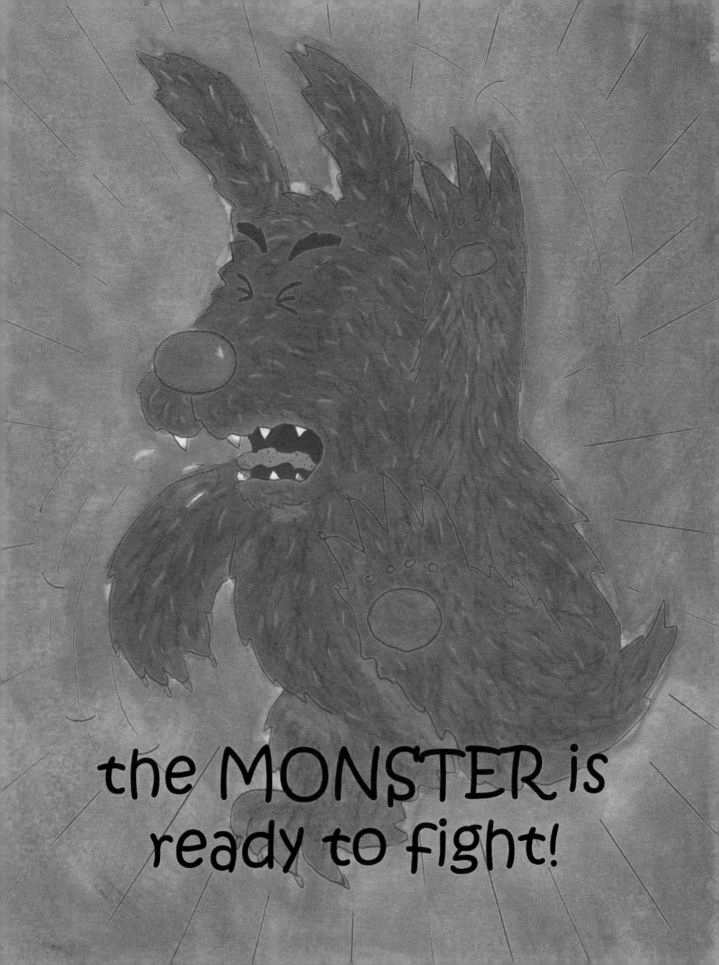

the MONSTER is
ready to fight!

My mom says the monster is anger and so

when I start to
get mad,

I should breathe
nice and slow.

My dad will say,
"Go to your room

and cool down."

My sister will leave and not want me around.

This isn't the kid that I am,

no! no! NO!

It's time for the MONSTER to go!

Getting angry is normal - we all feel that way

when someone is mean or we have a bad day.

And it isn't just kids who will sometimes get mad...

it's grandmas

and teachers

and neighbors

and dads.

Since anger is normal, then it must be true

that to keep it controlled,

there are things
I can do.

So if I can calm down when something goes wrong,

the MONSTER won't be quite so strong!

Now I'm making a plan

for when I get mad.

I'll write what I feel

to let out all that bad.

I'll talk to my parents

or find someone else,

and if no one's around,

then I'll talk to myself!

I'll take some deep breaths and then

I'll count to ten,

Calm and in charge is what I want to be..

The plan's really working

to help keep me straight.

It's been a few weeks now

and things are still great!

Like everyone, I still get angry sometimes,

but the difference,
it seems,

is the anger is
MINE.

No more feeling that goes from my toes to my eyes...

no more slamming of doors, or tantrums, or cries...

NO MORE monster INSIDE OF MY HEAD!

THE END

(I feel so much better now!)

28750117R00034

Made in the USA
Charleston, SC
19 April 2014